of
EASTER EGGS and
THINGS

By Nan Holcomb

Illustrated by Dot Yoder

JASON & NORDIC PUBLISHERS
HOLLIDAYSBURG, PENNSYLVANIA

"For the winter is past, the rain is over and gone. The flowers are springing up and the time of the singing of birds has come.
Yes, spring is here. The leaves are coming out, and the grapevines are in blossom."

Song of Solomon 2:11-13

"The Lord has really risen!"
Luke 24:34

Library of Congress Cataloging-in-Publication Data
Holcomb, Nan, date ___
    Of Easter eggs and things / by Nan Holcomb ; illustrated by Dot Yoder.
       p.cm.
    Summary: Six-year-old Ryan does not understand what bunnies and eggs
    have to do with Easter until his mother takes him to see all the signs of new life on
    the farm and explains about how Jesus rose in new life too.
    ISBN 0-944727-42-5 (alk. Paper)
       [1. Easter- -Fiction.] I. Yoder, Dot, date ___ -ill. II. Title.
PZ7.H6972 Of 2000
[E]- -dc21

                                                                        99-058702

ISBN 0-944727-42-5
Printed in the United States of America

For:

"Hey, Mom! Can we...may we buy some Easter egg stuff?" Ryan asked. "Can we? Please, Mom?"

"Please, Mom?" Anna asked.

"You don't even know about coloring Easter eggs," Ryan said. "You don't even remember! You were only one last year.

All you did was eat the color things."

"Did not!" Anna said and stuck out her tongue.

"Did so! And don't stick out your tongue!"

"Stop it! Both of you," Mom said. "Yes! You may get one."

"Hurry, and choose one so we can check out. The lady is waiting."

Ryan picked out a big package that had cups to match each color. It had little chicken designs and rabbit ears to put on the colored eggs.

What fun it would be! He could hardly wait until Easter!

Soon they had everything loaded into the van. "A stop at the bank and then home!" Mom said. "It won't take long now!"

On the bank drive-up window Ryan
noticed paper cut-outs of flowers and
Easter bunnies carrying baskets of eggs.
    "Why rabbits and eggs and flowers?"
he asked, but nobody heard him.

He rode quietly for a while, then he had to ask it! "Why do we color eggs anyway?"

"Why what?" Mom asked as they waited for the light to turn green.

"Why eggs? Why Easter eggs? Why Easter Bunnies and Easter eggs?"

"That is a lot of 'whys' even for you, Ryan," Mom said. "Because... because Jesus is alive and eggs are a sign of ...of...new life."

"Oh," Ryan answered. Just 'oh' because it really didn't make much sense.

He thought about it all the way home.

Eggs are eggs. Eggs are to eat with toast. Eggs are to put into cakes and things. Eggs are to color.

But how are they a sign of new life and what can they possibly have to do with Jesus?

Then he thought about rabbits. Rabbits are rabbits. Rabbits get into the garden and eat the plants. There are pretend stories about rabbits.

But, rabbits are just rabbits. And they can't carry eggs in baskets. How can rabbits be a sign of new life?

What can they have to do with Jesus?
He thought about it when he
helped put the groceries away.

He thought about it when he and
Anna had cookies and milk.

He thought about it when he
helped set the table for dinner.

    He even thought about it while
Dad asked the blessing.

    Dad said, "Amen."

    Ryan said, "I don't get it!"

    "What?" Mom and Dad both asked
at the same time. "What don't you get,
Ryan?"

"I don't know how eggs and rabbits are a sign of new life!"

"Hm-m-m..." Mom said. "I have an idea, but first...eat your dinner!"

After dinner Mom got right up from the table and went to the phone.

"Yes...yes," she said. "Tomorrow they'll start? Great! See you about 10:00! Thank you!" and she hung up. "You'll have a treat in the morning, Ryan! You'll know about signs of new life! I promise!"

The next morning Ryan bounded
out of bed, pulled on his jeans and
sweat shirt and ran downstairs for
breakfast.

Danny Dog helped him eat his toast
and egg so he could hurry through
breakfast.

He and Danny Dog waited and waited
on the porch for Mom and Anna.

At last they were all ready and on
their way. Ryan couldn't imagine where
they were going until they passed a horse
and buggy.

"Look! That's Mr. Hills' neighbor!"

"Oh, wow! We're going to Cackleberry Farm! Great!" Ryan yelled.

"Great!" Anna echoed.

Mr. Hill met them and lifted Anna
high in the air.

Anna yelled, "Do it again!"

Mrs. Hill brought each of them a warm cookie so Mr. Hill didn't have to do it again.

"Now for the surprise and you are just in time!" Mr. Hill said.

He led them into the small barn near the house.

There in a wire cage was a beautiful white mother rabbit. Snuggled up to her were four tiny pink bunnies without any fur.

"They aren't white and furry!"

"No," Mr. Hill said. "They're too young. They were just born."

"So!" Ryan said. "Bunnies can't carry Easter baskets!"

"The bunny and his gifts of eggs on Easter are lots of fun, but, I'd say this mother rabbit and her bunnies are a sign of new life in this old barn!" Mr. Hill said. "Come, I have something else to show you. Look through that door into

the garden. What do you see."

"Wow!" Ryan said.

"Wow," Anna echoed.

There in front of the fence, hundreds of yellow flowers nodded in the breeze.

"Another sign of new life in the spring." Mom said. "Remember the brown bulbs we helped plant last fall?"

"I remember! Oh, look!" Ryan yelled. "Look!"

"Look! Look!" Anna echoed.

There by the fence stood a mother sheep and her lamb.

"Hello, Myrtle," Mr. Hill called. "Come meet her new Easter lamb. He's only a few hours old."

Mr. Hill led them over to the fence. He held Anna up so she could reach over the fence and pet the soft woolly lamb.

"Another sign of new life?" Ryan asked. "But bunnies and lambs don't come from eggs!"

"Well, now I think it's time to answer that big egg question!" Mr. Hill

said and led the way into a small warm building.

Ryan looked all around. It was hot and stuffy and what was so special about a tray with hundreds of eggs!

Just then...Ryan heard a tiny crackling noise. He heard it again. Was it coming from the tray of eggs?

He stared at the eggs. There before his eyes, he saw a hole appear. Soon he saw another hole and then another. Wet little heads popped up.

"Peep! Peep! Peep!" they chirped and began hopping around. "Peep! Peep! Peep!" Soon they were fluffy and dry.

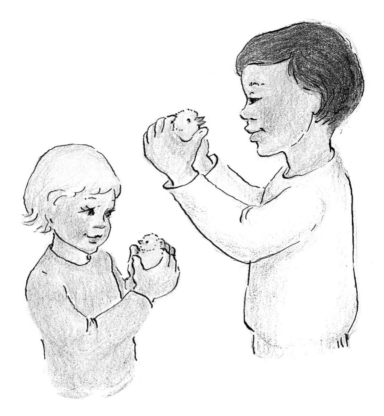

Mr. Hill put a chick into Ryan's hands and another one into Anna's.

"So soft and warm," Ryan said. "A new life in an egg! I get it! An egg is a sign of new life!"

Mom smiled. "We celebrate Easter with eggs because they help us remember that Jesus died and rose again in new life!

Coloring eggs makes them special for Easter!"

Back home that afternoon Ryan and Anna dipped eggs in the plastic cups. "This is a great way to get ready for Easter!" Ryan said.

"Ready for Easter!" Anna yelled and dropped the egg in the cup with a splash!

Early Easter morning, Ryan and Anna
ran downstairs. They found colored eggs
hiding everywhere and each found a big
Easter basket behind the sofa.

As Ryan put on his new clothes for
church, he thought about all the signs of
new life at Cackleberry Farm.

Later at church, Ryan looked at the flowers and at the happy faces around him. "Al-le-lu-ia," he sang. "lay-loo-yah!" Anna sang loudly and late!

Ryan whispered softly to God:

"Thank you, God, for the signs of new life at Easter, for Cackleberry Farm, the bunnies, the lamb, the chicks and flowers, for coloring Easter eggs and most of all, for Jesus.   Amen."